The Evening Walk

by Joanne Ryder
illustrated by Julie Durrell

A GOLDEN BOOK • NEW YORK
Western Publishing Company, Inc., Racine, Wisconsin 53404

One warm evening, Mama Skunk said to her children, "This is a lovely time to take a walk through the woods. Come Whisper, come Bell."

"Where are we going?" asked Whisper in his soft voice.

"Is it far?" asked his sister, Bell.

"Far enough," said Mama.

So the three skunks left their home and started their walk.

"Look at all the pretty lights," cried Bell. Her high voice rang through the quiet night.

"Those are stars," said Mama.

"Have you ever been to a star?" asked Whisper.

"Oh, no," said Mama. "They are too far away."

"Even for you, Mama?" asked Whisper.

"Yes," said Mama. "Even for me."

"Here's a little star," said Bell. "And it's not far at all."

She pointed to a tiny yellow light flickering in the bushes.

"I see some, too," called Whisper. Four tiny lights drifted over his head.

"Those are fireflies," said Mama. "They like to visit the woods on warm evenings, too."

As the family walked on, the woods grew darker and darker.

"What's that, Mama?" asked Whisper. He pointed to a big, dark shape far away.

"That's a mountain," said Mama.
"Can we go there?" asked Bell.
"The mountain is very far from here," said
Mama. "When you're bigger, we'll go there."

"Here's a mountain I can reach," said Bell. She climbed up a big pile of rocks.

"I think you've found a mountain just your size," said Mama.

"What can you see up there?" Whisper asked.

"I see you and Mama and the woods," Bell said, "and the bright stars far away."

The family continued their walk.

"Listen," Whisper said quietly. "Someone is breathing. Someone big."

"Don't be afraid," said Mama. "That's just the waterfall."

"It's very noisy," said Bell.

"The water moves so fast," said Whisper, watching it fall from the tall cliff. "Can we go up there?"

"Some night we will," said Mama. "But it's too far to visit tonight."

"I hear another waterfall," said Bell. "But it's a quiet one."

"You hear the stream," said Mama. "The water makes a soft sound as it moves over the rocks and the pebbles."

"Can we go there?" asked Whisper.
"Yes," said Mama. "We can all go there and get a drink. It isn't far."

Mama led Whisper and Bell to the stream. They all drank the cool water.

"Come along now," said Mama. "I have a special place to show you."

She took them to a clearing. They looked up and saw many stars in the sky. Then the moon came out from behind a cloud.

"Oh, Mama, look," cried Bell. "What's that?"

"It's the moon," said Mama.

"This is such a lovely spot," said Mama. "I
like to come here and watch the shiny moon
peek over the trees."

Whisper and Bell watched the moon rise
higher and higher.

Bell was the first to look down. "Look at all these moons," she cried. Near her head, four shiny circles were tucked in a little tree.

"Those are spider webs," said Mama. "The moonlight makes them glimmer in the dark."

Whisper and Bell liked this special part of the woods. They heard crickets chirping and frogs calling in deep voices. A soft breeze moved the grass ever so gently.

"This is a nice spot," said Bell.
"And it wasn't too far," said Whisper.
"No," said Mama, "it wasn't. But now it's getting late. Come along."

The family walked along the stream. They passed the waterfall and the mountain.

Suddenly Bell stopped. "They're gone," she said sadly. "All the fireflies are gone."

"They're resting now," said Mama. "It's time for fireflies to sleep. And very soon it will be time for small skunks to go to sleep, too."

"How much farther?" asked Bell.
"Only a few steps more," said Mama.
Then she led her sleepy children home
and to bed.